UNCERTAINTY PRINCIPLES

ALAN P. MARKS

Cover design copyright © 2025 by Niki Lenhart
nikilen-designs.com

Published by Paper Angel Press
paperangelpress.com

ISBN 978-1-969655-53-1 (Trade Paperback)

FIRST EDITION

10 9 8 7 6 5 4 3 2 1

UNCERTAINTY PRINCIPLES

T RY TELLING IT LIKE A STORY. That's what Susan said. Start with something happy.

'Once upon a time.' Isn't that how those things go?

1

Once upon a time, there was a family. A mother and a father, and a little girl and her older brother, and they all lived together—happily to all outward appearances —in a tiny house on the edge of a great forest.

Deep within that forest there lay a lake and, on the hottest days of summer, after their father (who was a woodcutter) came home, he would sometimes take the little girl and her older brother to swim in its cool, clear waters. On their way there, the girl would often run far ahead of her father and brother on the trail. Or slow down and let herself fall behind. The trail was twisty, and it never took long before a bend in the path would hide them from her and she could imagine she was by herself, alone in the wilds, off on some grand adventure. This never frightened the girl, though, because she knew it was only for pretend. The trail was clear and easy to follow, without any branches between their house and the lake. You could never lose yourself, at least not as long as you stayed on the trail. Not even a little girl.

And it felt like their own special, secret world, the trail and the lake and the woods in between. You had to pick your way through a thick wall of heavy brush behind their house before you broke onto the trail so—if you didn't already know it was there—you might never find it, or even think to look for it.

Once you'd made it through the brush, though, the trail was clear and ran both ways. The girl never knew where it went in the other direction, or if it really went anywhere at all. Or who might have made the trail in the first place, or why. For her, it was as if the only thing that existed was the two miles or so that led from their house to the lake. The idea that it was there for them and them alone and for no other reason, made perfect sense.

But then, she was just a very little girl.

•   •   •

I'm on my way to work and I manage to spill coffee all down my front when I get the call about dad. The hands-free is always too goddamn loud in the car and I can't ever figure out how to adjust the fucking thing. Small blessing that I've been nursing it for a while—stuck in morning rush hour traffic—so at least it isn't scalding anymore. Which means I'm only swearing a blue streak in my head, and not out loud when I pick up. It's not a number I recognize, so that's probably for the best.

Sgt. something-or-other from the State Police up in Maine, calling to give me the news that my father died. And to offer his "sincerest condolences."

Sincere. Right. He sounds stiff. Like he's reading off a script.

In my head, I'm picturing him sitting at his desk in his full statie glory, even though he's probably inside and none of that makes any sense. The Smokey the Bear hat I still remember they wore up there in Maine. The mirrored sunglasses cops wear everywhere it seems. The whole nine yards.

And stick-up-his-ass straight. All "Mr. Policeman" and everything.

Then there's me, stopped dead in traffic on the Garden State Parkway, sitting in a puddle of piss-warm coffee. Just fucking great.

Did I laugh out loud?

I might have laughed out loud.

I must have done something, because there's this long, awkward pause on the other end, to the point where I start to wonder if we've been cut off. Or maybe Sgt. Whatshisname decided to hang up on the crazy woman.

I probably laughed.

My mind can be a real asshole sometimes, and laughing when someone tells you that a couple of weeks ago the mailman happened to look through a window and saw your father slumped over in his chair and called 911? That's pretty much me all over.

"Inappropriate emotional response," Susan calls it. A "defense mechanism." A way to deflect, and to "avoid painful emotions by making light of the situation." Well, fuck 'em if they can't take an awkward and inappropriately timed joke.

In my defense, it's all a bit of a shock. I haven't heard from the man since the day mom loaded me and as much of our stuff as she could cram into that crappy little station wagon we used to own, and drove away.

The year Bobby disappeared.

Not a phone call. Not a letter. Not a birthday card. Nothing. Not for thirty-six *fucking* years.

And now this.

Of course, Sgt. … Clarke … that's it … he doesn't know any of that. But he also doesn't hang up. He just ignores my laughing at my dead dad and soldiers on. Good for him. I probably would have hung up.

Avoidance, Susan would call that. Yeah, that sounds like me.

Shut up, Susan.

Instead, he apologizes that it took so long to notify me, but they'd had a hard time tracking down the next of kin.

That would be me. Next and only.

I'm kind of surprised/impressed they found me at all, to be honest, since mom changed my last name along with hers when she left dad and went back to her maiden name. Add two more married names of my own on top of that, and some people might say it was almost like I was *trying* to hide. There certainly can't have been a very clear trail to follow between dad and me, that's for damn sure.

So, kudos Maine State Police.

I guess.

There's another pause (I know I didn't laugh this time), and now I'm picturing him flipping back and forth through his file on dad and seeing the bit about the ex-wife and *two* kids—a son as well as a daughter. But he only pauses for a second, so maybe not.

It was an overdose, he says. Dilaudid. For pain. They found it along with a bunch of other prescriptions. Chemo drugs, mostly. Pancreatic cancer. End stage. They were calling the overdose accidental, but something in his voice made me wonder.

Not that it matters a hell of a lot when you get to "end stage."

He can't say, exactly, how long dad's been gone, though. Beyond when the mailman found him, the best they can tell is maybe two or three weeks before that. Time of death, he says, is hard to pin down the longer you get from it. If not for a certified letter from the power company threatening to cut off service if he didn't pay his bill, they still might not have discovered … my father.

I grin at that. He almost slipped there. But it's probably cop 101 that you're not supposed to talk about "the body" when notifying the "grieving family." Visions of decomposing corpses and all that.

At any rate, if the mailman hadn't had to go up and knock on the door for a signature, who knows how long it might have been before anyone noticed anything? For me, dad would still be "alive."

Not sure how I feel about any part of that.

He's kind of like that cat in the box, the one where, until you open it, there's no way to know if the cat's alive or dead so, somehow, it's both. I never really got that before. I'd always thought, well, wouldn't the cat know?

Cue morbid dad joke.

What do you call a lonely old man living by himself when he swallows a bottle of pills?

Schrodinger's Dad.

Ba-dum-bump.

Depends on your point of view, I suppose. For dad, it's been maybe a month or so. Only he knows for sure and, like the cat, he's not saying much. For the police and the mailman, it's been about two weeks.

For me, only a few minutes.

Or maybe thirty-six years. As good as, anyway.

My own personal uncertainty principle.

•　　　•　　　•

Next to the trail on the way to the lake stood an old deadfall, a giant pine that had snapped near the bottom a long, long time ago, perhaps in a storm or perhaps only under its own weight. Despite its great size, though, it hadn't fallen all the way to the ground but had instead wedged itself at an angle between the other trees. To the girl, it looked like a bridge up into the sky and, if you were brave enough, you might walk up that bridge, up into the treetops high above. The little girl knew she would never have been able to do it, though. She thought herself brave, but she knew she wasn't nearly brave enough for that.

But then, their father never let them climb up onto the tree, not even a little ways, because you never knew what could cause everything to come crashing down. He was a woodcutter, after all, and knew about such things. Her brother pouted at this, but the girl was secretly glad because she didn't have to admit she might be afraid.

Whenever they came to that old, fallen pine, which marked almost exactly the halfway point between their little house and the lake, their father would always say in his deep but quiet voice, "It's all downhill from here children," and laugh because they knew that the trail was perfectly flat from the house to the lake and back. It was simply his way of telling his children that, for every step they took from then on, there would be that much less of the journey ahead than lay behind.

•   •   •

"You should try writing things down," Susan says.

It's our first session since I told her my father died.

"You don't always have to talk to someone *else* about what you're going through. Sometimes just opening up to *yourself* about those things can help."

In all the years I've been seeing her, this is the first time we've even come close to talking about dad. I talk about *mom* a lot. Like, a LOT a lot. She was a real piece of work, my mother. Not that she didn't have her reasons. Then again, I've got her beat, two ex-husbands to one, so maybe I'm a piece of work, too.

Bobby? I never talk about Bobby.

That I have … had … a father is a given. He existed in theory, at least. Biologically speaking, he sort of had to.

Susan doesn't even know I *had* a brother.

Yeah, I know. Avoidance and all that. I get it.

"And it doesn't have to be like a diary or anything," Susan goes on. "I mean, that can work too, but sometimes that can still feel a little too real. Too raw. So, you can try maybe writing it like a story. Something made up. Like it happened to someone else entirely. It might sound silly, but that can often be enough to give a person the emotional distance they need. Can make it easier.

8

"And trick yourself," she says. "Don't try going straight at whatever it is your mind is shying away from. You'll just keep on doing it. What you want to do is sort of sneak up on the sore spots.

"Start with a *happy* story."

I have to give it to her. She's doing a good job hiding her excitement. If I didn't know her …

But when I called her yesterday to tell her the news, and that I had to cancel for next week so I could drive up to Maine and deal with things, I could almost hear the "holyshitholyshitholyshit" running through her head. The only thing she said, though, was that she'd had a cancellation for the next day and why didn't I stop in. All calm and casual like. As if she wasn't getting right back on the phone after we hung up to reschedule whoever it was she just bumped.

And when I got here, she only asked me how I was handling everything and then let me ramble on for a while about getting time off from work for the next week or so. About packing for fall weather in Maine. Meaningless stuff.

White noise.

Now, she's fishing around in her desk. "I think I've got an old journal kicking around in a drawer here somewhere. You could take it with you if you wanted. If I can find it, that is."

Real subtle, Susan.

We lie to each other like that. She pretends not to notice that I've got baggage I won't talk about. I pretend not to notice that she notices, or that I can see how, in her own way, she's always poking at the edges of that baggage.

Or that there's a spot on the cover of the "old, unused" little notebook that's still sticky from where the price tag was just peeled off.

She pretends that I don't know exactly what she's doing.

It kind of works for us.

•   •   •

Some days—special days if their father got home early enough and if it wasn't so hot that all they wanted to do was swim—they would leave the path at the old fallen pine and head deeper into the woods. To their other secret place.

Back in the distant past, thousands and thousands and thousands of years ago, the whole town and everything around it as far as the eye could see had been covered in vast sheets of ice. Glaciers, the little girl's teacher had told them at school. She also told them that, when the glaciers melted away thousands and thousands and thousands of years ago, they left behind gigantic stones that they had picked up far away to the north and had carried all the way down to here.

The girl almost raised her hand, then, to tell her teacher how they had a lot of those in the woods right behind their house, but she stopped herself because she was afraid the other children might want to go there to see, and that would mean they would also learn about the trail and the lake.

If they did, none of it would be secret or special any longer.

•　　•　　•

I'm not in much of a hurry, so driving up to Maine takes the better part of two days. With enough coffee, if I pushed it I could maybe do it in one. Maine's a fucking big state, though. I always forget that. And I need to go way up north. Plus, showing up in the dead of night doesn't seem like the brightest of ideas.

I haven't thought about the old house in forever and, the whole way there, I try remembering as best I can, going over it and over it in my head. My first ex would tell me I'm being obsessive about it, and to give it goddamn rest. But then he always was that particular kind of asshole.

Besides, it's not like there's much else to do while I drive.

It feels a bit like doing a jigsaw puzzle. One where you lost the box and now only have the vaguest idea of the picture. At first, all I can get are the basics. The edge pieces. A little white two-story box of a house with a one-story extension off the back. Graying clapboards showing here and there through the peeling paint.

The rest of it takes longer, but I've got plenty of time. By morning of the second day when I cross the big bridge into Maine at Kittery, I've got most of it filled in.

Green shutters bracket the front windows of the house, the ones facing the road, one window on the second floor, two on the first with a door in-between. One of the shutters on the upstairs window—that one had been my room—hangs a little crooked. Damage from some storm, maybe. It never got fixed, but it never came off, either. It was just always that way. I never knew it any different.

The door is the same dark green as the shutters. A door no one ever uses. In Maine everyone uses the back. Front doors are a kind of architectural appendix, a vestigial organ that might have once served some purpose but not anymore. A place to hang decorations for whatever holiday season it might be, and then forget to take them down until long after the holiday has passed.

The house is set back a decent ways from the road and a long, narrow, dirt driveway wraps around the right side to a little detached garage out behind. Inside, the garage was always cluttered to where even a kid could barely squeeze through it. The closest it ever came to having something parked inside was when dad would shove the crap back far enough (bitching about it the whole time) to nose his pickup in so he could tinker with the engine under cover.

No matter how much he bitched, though, the clutter always crept back.

A big dooryard out in front of the house. *Doah-yahd.* A huge elm tree right in the middle. Other than that, everything is open facing the road, but smaller trees and scrub brush wrap around the property on the other three sides, isolating it from the rest of the world, even if there are neighbors not more than a quarter mile up the road in either direction.

Behind the house, nothing but trees and trees for miles. There's a little pond a couple miles back in those woods where we'd go swimming in the summers.

The lawn is neatly mowed, always, although there wouldn't have been anyone to take care of that for the last month or so, I guess. Only it's late enough in the year now, and the days cold enough and short enough, that the grass wouldn't be growing much at this point anyways. Besides, with no one to rake them up and bag them, it would mostly be buried under a thick carpet of leaves from the elm. It still looks like late summer in Jersey, at least for a little while longer, but the drive north is like a two-day time-lapse of the changing seasons where you can watch everything shift from greens to a mix of bright reds and oranges and yellows, and finally to the uniform dull, dead, brown of empty branches.

Even after crossing the border from New Hampshire, though, I've got hours left ahead of me. So, once I get that picture in my head, as clear and complete as I can make it, I go back and start over. Again and again like a game as the miles tick past, piecing in some new little detail I've only just remembered each time (okay, okay, maybe I'm obsessing a *little*).

The sagging awning over the back door on the side of the one-story addition.

The faded Tot Finder sticker in the upstairs window.

The mailbox on a post at the end of the driveway out by the road.

The stacked cinderblock "steps" to the front door.

A detail here. A detail there.

But only on the outside.

I'm not ready to go in yet.

•   •   •

On those days when the father led his children away from the trail and deeper into the woods, he never let the little girl go on ahead or fall behind because, without a clear trail to follow, anyone, be it a little girl, or her older brother, or even a grown man could become lost and never find their way back again.

But the father, who knew the woods, always led them without fail.

And, once at their special place, they climbed. Many of the stones were small enough (though still giant to the girl) and broken apart with lots of places for little fingers and little toes, so that she could climb them by herself. The biggest, though, which looked to the girl more like a hill than a stone, was too tall for her to climb on her own.

So, after her older brother had had a turn, and had climbed up and then back down again, the little girl's father would help her up the crevice in the side of the giant rock where it had split a long, long time ago. Where she was able, he would let her go by herself, finding spots for her little fingers and little toes, climbing along with her to protect her if she slipped. Where she needed help, he would move her hands where they needed to go. Or boost her from behind so that she could get to a spot that might have been just out of her reach. And where there was no other way, she would turn and face him and wrap her arms around his neck and hold tight while he worked his way to a spot where she might go on again by herself for a ways.

Until they made it to the very top, where her father would stand there beside her for a time, before climbing back down far enough so he was out of sight and the girl could stand alone on top of the giant stone that seemed to her more like a hill.

And if it wasn't as high as if she climbed the old pine bridge up into the treetops, it still felt, to the girl, higher than she had ever been before, and she felt brave.

Once upon a time.

•　　　•　　　•

Except, when I get there, the shutters are blue, not green. Blue.

So is the front door.

Not some in-between blue-green mix. Not teal, or aqua, or "Caribbean Blue" like in the song. A deep, dark, unequivocable blue.

Well, shit.

And all I can do is sit and stare, my hands clenching the steering wheel because every time I take them off, they start shaking and I can't seem to make them stop. I throw the car into park but leave the engine running. Partly because I'm seriously considering turning the fuck around and driving straight back home. Or, at the very least, seeing if there's a motel in town. There's no way in hell I'm staying here tonight.

Everything else about the place—those puzzle pieces I've spent the better part of two days flipping over and slotting into place—they fit almost perfectly, right down to the crooked shutter on the upstairs window. That's what should really be screwing me up, just how unchanged it is, the house, the yard, the big elm. Like time more or less *stopped* here the day we left.

I don't much *like* that idea. Kind of sad, really, thinking about dad marking time here. But at least I can process that. Can understand it.

The front yard—blanketed in leaves the way I imagined it would be—seems smaller, maybe. As if the undergrowth surrounding the house has been slowly inching its way forward year by year, the woods taking back what once belonged to it. But the house feels like it shrank, too, and I know *that* can't be true. Sometimes things just look that way when you grow up.

And what does it matter? Who gives a shit if the shutters are blue or not? Or the door. It shouldn't make *any* difference. At all. An utterly meaningless and stupid fucking detail.

But I was so *sure* they'd been green.

Even sitting here in the driveway staring right at them, I can't make it fit. I close my eyes and try to picture the house and to *remember* them being blue, but all I can see in my mind's eye are dark green shutters and a dark green door.

Until I open them again.

I could lie to myself. Say they must have been painted sometime in the last three plus decades. That would make sense, wouldn't it? I haven't been here in forever, and things change. Only I can see that isn't true. The paint is faded and patchy in places with enough rust showing through on the door that I can see it from the car. None of it has seen a coat of paint in a long, long time.

Besides, at some point during those years, the balance tipped over from the house being mostly white with some graying wood showing through where the paint had begun to peel, to mostly gray, covered here and there with flecks of white.

Who leaves the rest of the house like that, but goes to the trouble of repainting shutters and doors?

No one, that's who.

I *remember* them as green, but they have to have always *been* blue.

If I can't trust *that* memory ...

2

*O*nce upon a time, a little girl followed her father into the forest.

Storm clouds darkened the late afternoon sky—a kind of magic that transformed day into dusk—and winds swirled the rain about the girl as she crept along in secret, the water running down her face like tears.

The woodcutter carried the boy in his arms and, though they would have both been soaked through and heavy with the rain, he was a large man and held his son as if the boy weighed nothing, cradling the body closely to himself. And that was how the little girl knew that her older brother must certainly be dead. He would have thought himself too grown up by far, and would never have allowed their father to carry him that way, as if he were a child.

•　　　•　　　•

Come to find out, in Maine, if a body isn't claimed within fifteen days, it's considered "abandoned." Actual fucking law.

After that, the funeral home can do pretty much whatever the hell it wants. Embalm and refrigerate it. Bury it.

Cremate it.

I'd never considered that. Who would?

I don't know if I even *wanted* to see him one last time. Would I recognize him? If I can't remember the color of a goddamned door …

Part of me is relieved. And part of me is pissed. I just can't tell what that second part is pissed at. Not having the option? Or at myself because I'm secretly glad that now I don't have to make that decision for myself?

The only thing I'm sure of is that it's a good thing I drove to the funeral home from the motel instead of walking the mile or so through town like I almost did. I never imagined I might actually be taking him home with me, like I'd popped out to pick up an order of take out.

Fun fact. When someone is cremated, their ashes don't automatically come in an urn. There's always an urn on tv shows and in the movies, so you kind of think that's how it goes. But you have to pay extra for that, and an urn can run you anywhere from $50 up to three or four hundred or more depending on what it's made of or how fancy it is.

I'd killed some time in the hotel between day one and day two of the drive googling shit on my phone.

There'd been nothing on TV.

You can get some that are truly hideous from Walmart online, it turns out, but even those will set you back like a hundred bucks.

Mom probably would have loved those.

But if you don't want to pay anything extra, they come in a cardboard box with a plastic bag of ashes inside.

So … I put the box in the trunk. Sandwiched in between the spare and a couple of bags of old clothes I keep forgetting to drop off at Goodwill.

It feels wrong. Disrespectful bordering on sacrilegious—not that I've set foot in a church in a while.

Except the only thing I can think is that, if I put him up front with me and then got into an accident on the drive out to the house, I'd end up having to vacuum him out of the carpet of my Corolla and I'd always worry that I didn't get everything.

Of course, I'm assuming it *is* him in the box. Some things you have to take on faith, I suppose. And I don't have any reason to think otherwise. But, for all I really know, the funeral home gave me a box full of floor sweepings. How could I tell the difference?

The box they give you is smaller than you'd think. Maybe 8 x 10 and not more than five inches tall. Like a small Amazon box (and, yeah, you can buy urns there, too). Surprisingly heavy, though. But then he was a big man. Not just big in the hazy memories of nine-year-old me, because everyone is giant when you're that young. He was at least a head taller than my mother, and much wider. Cancer wouldn't have taken *all* of that away.

Ashes to ashes, etc., etc.

Which is the other thing they don't tell you. It's not really ashes. Ashes don't weigh much of anything. The box is heavy because it's mostly bone fragments they have to grind up after everything else—everything that matters most—has been burned away.

The call them "cremains."

Ugh. To every part of that.

Thanks for that, Internet.

•   •   •

The woodcutter did not see his daughter following behind, despite the brightly colored raincoat and boots she wore over the pajamas her father had dressed her in earlier. She was hidden by the rain, and by the man's grief. If he had seen her, he surely would have made her take the path back to their little house at the forest's edge.

Yet, despite the risk of discovery, she followed as closely as she dared. The trail was twisty and, if she fell behind, it would be too easy to lose sight of him. If that were to happen, and if he should leave the trail, she might never know. Still, the girl almost missed it when her father turned by the old fallen pine. If not for the snap of a broken branch and the barest glimpse of movement through the trees and through the rain, she would have sped along the trail towards the lake, trying in vain to catch up to him again.

·   ·   ·

Once I've finally worked up the nerve to go back to the house and actually go inside this time, I walk through the place in a bit of a daze. But only the downstairs.

I have no desire to go up to my old bedroom.

Bobby's and my rooms were made by putting up a dividing wall and cutting one medium-size bedroom into two shoebox-sized ones. If I was a boy, we probably would have shared.

There was only one door in from the tiny upstairs hallway, though, and since Bobby was older, he got the privacy and I had to suffer him always walking though the corner of my room to get to his.

They're both probably empty now. Or packed full with junk. But I've got this irrational fear that, if I go upstairs, I'll discover that neither of them has changed. That my father just closed the door to the hall and never opened it again. That *I* would open it only to discover dirty clothes scattered across the floor, and toys that there hadn't been enough room in the car to take with us. Blankets still messed up from when my mother dragged me out of bed the morning we left.

That particular box I'm just as happy to leave unopened.

Get out of my head, Susan.

Details come back to me as I move from room to room. Little things. The color of the kitchen cabinets. The flower pattern of the linoleum on the kitchen floor. The dining table that had been barely big enough for the four of us. The ugly-ass wallpaper in the living room. The couch. His chair.

The place feels haunted.

I can't tell if I'm the ghost.

It's like re-reading a book you once knew, but so long ago you can't remember the details. Can remember reading it in the first place. Then, the more you flip through the pages now, the more it comes back, each part familiar to as you go, even if you couldn't have called any of it to mind before.

Some things are different, but they're expected things. Explainable things. Signs of the passage of time. The wallpaper has faded and yellowed and started to peel in the corners. The linoleum has worn from years of feet scuffing across it, though the pattern is still clear enough around the edges. A new, modern television sits on a stand in the living room where there was once this huge beast of a console TV. Hand towels cover the armrests of my father's chair and, when I lift the corner of one, I can see where the original fabric has worn almost completely away underneath, exposing the stuffing inside.

A stack of cardboard boxes has piled up in the corner of the dining room. A smaller stack in the living room.

The empty cigarette cartons in the recycling bin are new.

That there *is* a recycling bin is new.

There's plenty of food left in the kitchen cupboards, and I heat myself up a can of soup on the stove and find some crackers to go along with it. They're stale but, crumbled up in the soup, they'll be fine. Not much of a meal, but the act of doing something both familiar, yet also something that—for me—has no connection to this particular place … it settles my nerves. Brings up no memories. Rings no alarms.

I ate countless meals in this house, but have never *cooked* one here before.

I take the bowl into the dining room and set it on the table and, to pass the time and distract myself while I eat, I pull the dust-covered box off the top of the stack in the corner to look through whatever might be inside. At some point, I'm going to have sort through all this crap, anyway.

Newspapers. Old newspapers. Thirty-plus year-old newspapers. So much for settled nerves.

•   •   •

Certain of where they must be going now, but also knowing she might never find her way there on her own, the girl crept even closer behind her father and brother. She was not burdened as he was and the damp ground and falling rain shrouded her footsteps, so she made no stray noises that might have given herself away.

She was, after all, a very little girl.

Eventually, they came to their other special place in the forest, the place of the stones, and the girl hid herself behind a tree and watched as her father climbed the largest of them, the one that had always looked to her more like a hill than a stone. The one she would sometimes stand on top of and feel brave.

It was a hard climb, burdened as he was with the body of his son, and he stopped often to rest. A smaller, weaker man might not have managed. Eventually, though, the woodcutter reached the very top and disappeared over the edge. From where she stood, still hiding herself behind a tree, the girl could no longer see either of them.

The little girl would never see her older brother again.

•   •   •

I've long since done my own digging, of course—as soon as I was old enough, and as soon I could hide what I was doing from my mother. Old papers on microfilm at the library at first, and then, eventually, the Internet. But nothing like this. None of the little local publications where the story held on for so much longer and that were filled with more than just reporting the basic facts. Filled, at first, with an outpouring of support for the family, but later with rumor and suspicion and as close as you could get to outright accusation without facing a libel charge. And, after word got out that my mother had left and taken me with her, more than a few crossed over that line.

Half a dozen boxes, all but the top one packed full, and I sit there for hours reading through the stories in every last one, pausing at one point to find an old Coleman lantern when I realize that it's grown dark enough that I'm having trouble seeing the words on the page. Fucking power company followed through on their threat to shut off the power.

As if this wasn't bad enough in the light of day.

Pushed aside, my dinner—such as it is—has congealed into a cold, tomatoey paste. Not that I've got much of an appetite anymore. It disappeared almost as soon as I opened the first box, so, no loss there.

Every newspaper in the boxes lies folded open to some story about the missing boy or about his family, all of them more or less in order from the bottom box on up. Whenever my father stumbled across a new one, he'd add it to the growing pile. Paper on top of paper. Box on top of box.

I have no idea why he would have wanted to keep them.

I start at the beginning, pulling the box out from the bottom of the pile and flipping it over, dumping the papers on the table so I can read them all in order. Get the whole story from start to finish.

Not that there was ever any real ending to it.

Early on, the stories came almost daily, sometimes from several different newspapers with the same date. Front page stories, or near to it at first, mostly using different words to say more or less the same things. Stories about search parties, and pleas for information, and offers of rewards put up by local businesses. Pictures of Bobby in a lot of those early stories, usually his 8th grade school photo, but also a few others that looked familiar. Pictures from birthday parties or cookouts or just from around the house. Candids. My mother must have given them those. She had scrapbooks full. She took all of those with us when we left.

Later, when the story pushed its way back into the front pages again, they added pictures of my father alongside those same old ones of Bobby. Again, there were pleas for information, and stories about searches, but now those searches were happening in other places, places out in the deep woods, places where my father worked crews cutting timber.

Those stories were from around the time mom and I left, more or less.

I wonder if the papers got the pictures of dad from my mother, too. I couldn't say. Any pictures of him that might have once been in her scrapbooks, she'd thrown out a long time ago.

I'd hated her for that.

Towards the end of the boxes, a month might go by between the dates on the papers, and those almost all local ones. Those stories were little more than brief updates, buried somewhere way in the back pages, and the news was always that there *was* no news. The last story from the fall of '88 announced that the state police were ceasing any active search for Bobby. The case would remain open but, unless new leads presented themselves, there wasn't anything more they could do.

After that, nothing. So, a little over a year and a half from start to finish, before the world moved on to other things and the missing boy was mostly forgotten.

•   •   •

In time—how long the girl could not exactly say, though it had felt to her like ages—her father appeared again at the edge of the stone. Unburdened now, he began to make his way slowly back down. The girl knew then that she must go, or else risk being seen. She did not want her father to know she had followed him into the forest or that she had seen where he had gone and why. So, turning herself back the way they had come, or at least the direction from which she believed they had come, she hurried through the trees and away from her father. Even if she did not go back exactly the same way, she thought that, in time, she must surely find the trail again.

How easy it would have been for the little girl to lose herself in the wilds for real that day.

•   •   •

By the time I put the last newspaper back into the top of its box—back the way I found them, as if I was never here—all I want to do is sleep. Or cry. Or scream. Or maybe a bit of all three. But the closer I got to the end, the more it crept its way into the back of my mind that this *wasn't* the end. Because, when I first wandered through the house, I'd also seen a smaller stack of boxes tucked in the corner behind my father's chair. I look through the archway into the living room, but the lantern's light doesn't reach that far, and the room is dark. I can see them there, anyway. In my head. Waiting. Only a couple, and smaller than the others, but still.

Part of me doesn't think I can face reading through even more stories about Bobby and my father. My eyes are so tired from reading for so long and by lantern light that they physically hurt, and I can feel the beginnings of a headache coming on. A bad one.

Plus, that whole sleeping and crying and screaming thing.

But I'm also pretty sure I won't get any fucking sleep not knowing what's in those two extra boxes that he, for some reason, kept apart from the rest. There weren't any noticeable gaps in the stories in the ones I already looked through, only a slow but steady loss of interest in a scandal that never ended up going anywhere. Until it just sort of … faded away.

My mind can be a real asshole sometimes. I may have mentioned that.

And a fickle bitch, too. With some things, like my old bedroom, it will let me go on my merry way. Let me ignore it and move on. With others, it pokes and pokes and pokes until I break down and do whatever the hell it wants me to.

Part of me is crossing my fingers that it's just where the old man stashed his porn. I can be creeped out for a minute, and maybe a little bit sad for him, and then I can go to sleep.

Only, sitting on the couch a few minutes later, looking down into the first box, it takes a while to realize what I'm looking at. Maybe I'm too damn tired. Or maybe I'd been so sure it was going to be more newspapers that, when it's not, it doesn't quite register.

Envelopes. Nothing but envelopes. All lined up nice and neat. I pull open the flaps of the other box and more of the same. Between the two boxes, there must be hundreds, each one sealed and stamped and ready to mail. Each one with my father's name and return address in the corner, in the rough, blocky handwriting that by some trick of memory I recognize as his. The only thing missing is an address to send them to.

But every single one has my name on it.

Cue stupid post office joke.

Something … something … dead letter office.

Slowly and carefully, I close first one box and then the other, folding the flaps back together to seal them up again. Just as slowly and just as carefully, I stack them back up the way they'd been.

And then I shove them as hard as I can with both feet, sending them tumbling to the other side of the room. The seam on one gives way, leaving a trail of those offending envelopes spread across the floor behind it like a scar. Or an accusation.

Fuck.

•   •   •

And yet, the girl did not lose herself. Coming to the trail much further along towards the lake than the old fallen pine, the little girl turned towards home and ran as fast as she was able, all the way there for fear that, if her father went straight to the pine, he might get ahead of her and arrive at the house before she did.

By the time the girl left the trail again behind the little house, the hour was late and true night was beginning to fall. Despite the gloom, no light came from the windows, so she felt certain that she had made it home before her father. Her mother, at work in the nearby town, would not be home for hours yet.

Still, she crept quietly into the house, hiding her boots and raincoat in the back of the closet so they wouldn't give away that she had been out in rain. Then, going swiftly up the stairs to her room where her father had left her, she replaced her damp clothes with dry ones, and climbed back beneath the covers of her bed where he had left her, what seemed like such a long time ago. Eventually, she heard the door to the house open and close, heard her father's heavy footsteps on the stairs. Feigning sleep, she heard the door to her room open and, after a time, gently close again.

She may have fallen asleep then for real, or she may have not. But, in time, the girl heard the voices of her mother and father somewhere in the house below, though she could not hear what they might have said to each other.

And they were all there. An unhappy little family. A mother and a father and a little girl, living together in a tiny house right on the edge of a great forest.

•   •   •

Sometime around midnight—the mess cleaned up; the broken box taped back together as best I can—I finally curl up on the couch to try to sleep. As exhausted as I am, though, sleep won't come, and I lie there listening to the quiet hiss of the lantern. I can't bring myself to turn it off. Things can creep up on you in the dark. Whether they're actually there or not.

I should have gone back to the motel but, now that I'm here, I feel trapped. And I can't explain why. I tell myself that, if I did go to the motel, I'd only end up lying there, wide awake, thinking about this place anyway. So, why bother? I can get a shitty night's sleep here as easily as anywhere. No need to drive somewhere else to do it.

But none of that is really true. I don't know what is.

I roll over onto my side, though, and face the back cushions of the couch so at least I won't feel the pull to open my eyes every few minutes to look at his chair sitting there on the other side of the room. Or the boxes sitting next to it.

Would I see him there in the dim light if I did? Would he be slumped over the way the mailman found him, or would he be staring back at me, some impossible to read look in his eyes?

I used to love that fucking chair. The back stiff and too straight, the armrests too far apart for little arms to rest on comfortably, not both at the same time. And the cushions had lumps in all the wrong places.

In every reasonable way you could measure it, the couch was better.

But I was "grown up" when I sat in dad's chair.

3

*O*nce upon a time, it was not once upon a time.
It was the time, and the time after, and the time after that.
The first time, the little girl was only eight.

She won't remember that she was eight. Not really. There will be many things that she will no longer remember. Things she will choose not to remember.

But, in later years, she will know she must have been eight, because she will remember her ninth birthday and how her best friend Margie spilled her punch on herself at the party. And how, even though it was mean, they had all laughed, even the little girl who had been Margie's best friend, because it looked like she'd peed her pants. And how they weren't really best friends anymore after that.

And that was after, because it had been red punch, and the little girl had suddenly thought how it looked like Margie was bleeding down there … and how the girl had stopped laughing then … and how she never really wanted to play with Margie much after that day so not being best friends anymore had been sort of okay.

All she will remember from the first time is that she didn't understand what he was doing. Or why.
And not feeling brave.

•   •   •

To get to the trail I have to pick my way through the bushes behind the house. Took a lot less effort when I was little—fewer scratches to show for it and considerably less swearing on my part—but it isn't long before I break through and onto the path. And not as long as I remember it being from there to the deadfall.

The half-fallen tree finally collapsed the rest of the way at some point. Broke apart higher up and came crashing down a long time ago. You can tell by how the rotting wood has sunk into the soft ground and how the undergrowth has sprung up around it. Give it another thirty-six years and you might never know it had been here at all. For now, though, it still clearly marks where I need to turn off and head deeper into the woods.

"It's all downhill from here," I whisper over my shoulder to nobody.

I don't sound very convincing.

Hitching the old backpack I found in a closet at the house a little higher up on my shoulders, I try to point myself in more or less the same direction I remembered going all those years ago.

The police must have searched these woods back then. They must have found the trail. But they never found Bobby. It's too far off the beaten path. Literally. And it was our secret place. We never told anyone about it.

I find it easy enough now. Even after all this time, that one rock seems enormous to me, and towers over the others.

I still have no clue how he climbed it back then, in the rain and carrying Bobby. I can barely manage it with my hands free on a sunny day.

Up on top, it only takes a little feeling around before a discover a notch where the two bigger sections of the fragmented boulder come together. Smaller rocks fill the notch, almost as if they've been deliberately placed there. Patches of lichen cover everything, and moss fills the cracks between the stones. There could be an opening underneath. Or there could be nothing.

There's not really much else for options.

If I was smart, I would have thought to bring tools with me, but this hasn't been my best couple of days so all I can do is work by hand. By the time I pull out some of the larger pieces of moss and pry one of the stones free to reveal a patch of darkness beneath, my fingers are raw. Not quite bleeding yet but, between the digging and the climb up, close to it.

The opening I manage to make is small, barely big enough to fit my hand through, if I had any desire to reach in and feel around. Which I don't. Like … at all. It looks deep, though. I can't see anything inside, but then I don't have much desire to do that either.

Shrugging off the backpack, I take out the box from inside. Then the bag from inside the box. The hole in between the rocks is more than big enough to empty the contents into it.

It feels like maybe I should say something. Seems like the kind of thing you're supposed to do at moments like this. Only, I can't imagine what. I stuff the empty bag and box back into the pack, and the rock back into the hole I pulled it out of. Piece the bits of moss back into the cracks as best I can. Not a very convincing job of covering my traces but, in a few months, I doubt you'd be able to tell anyone had ever been here.

•   •   •

And once upon a time comes a time when the little girl says no. She says it without thought. Without intent.

She does not feel brave.

She feels anger. And maybe, just maybe, hate.

He stands, blocking her door, blocking her escape, and in her fury the little girl pushes at him. But he is so much larger than her.

He will always be larger than her and as hard as she pushes, it does no good. And yet, he hits her anyway. He has hit her before, and he knows where to hit and how hard, so that it will leave no marks. He is clever and understands that he needs to be careful of that. Still, it is more than hard enough to hurt.

Only this time the girl does not feel the pain of it through the sudden and unfamiliar and overpowering rage that surges through her body and sends her running past his surprised and too-slow grasp. Into the hallway outside of her room and down the stairs.

•   •   •

Those two fucking boxes, still sitting right there when I get back to the house. Right where I'd left them the night before. They might hold every answer I've ever wanted.

The questions? They're almost always why, and why me?

If I knew, I could blame somebody.

I want to blame somebody.

Somebody other than myself.

The rational part of my mind knows none of it was my fault. It couldn't have been. I was just a little girl.

The asshole parts? That's a different story.

The asshole parts are willing to blame anybody.

And they ask different questions.

•   •   •

The knife is in her hands as if by magic. It must be magic—a cruel and malicious kind, perhaps, but magic nonetheless—because she has no memory (and never will) of taking it down from where it hung from the wall of the kitchen, barely within her reach. It is simply and suddenly there, gripped tightly in her trembling hands.

Does he not see the knife as he reaches for her where she stands in the middle of the room (for the little girl has decided she will run no longer)? Does she, in her anger and hatred, push the knife towards him? Or does she simply hold it steady as he, perhaps unknowingly, perhaps not, steps into it?

The little girl does not know any of these things.

The woman that she will one day become will not know.

All either of them will ever know, and will never be able to forget, is the sudden rush of warmth and wetness over their hands, and the high-pitched sound he makes as he falls to the ground, a sound that will always remind her of air being slowly let out of a balloon.

That, and looking up to see her father standing in the doorway, his eyes wide, home from work early because it wasn't safe to work in the woods in the rain.

•　　　•　　　•

Questions like, why did my father hide the body? Why did he let everyone suspect him? Was it to protect me, or was it for some other reason?

Why did he let my mother suspect him—let her take me away?

Did she know the truth? If she did, what was it that made her grow to hate my father so completely?

Or is the truth something else entirely? Something other than anything I've ever imagined.

And how could Bobby do what he did?

•　　　•　　　•

Her father does not say anything. He does not go to his son. Perhaps he knows it is already too late, or perhaps he understands.

Everything.

Instead, he goes to the girl. He is a large man and towers over her. She flinches away, as if expecting him to strike her down for the horrific and unforgivable thing she has done, but he does not. He only takes from her hands the knife that she does not even realize she still holds, and sets it aside. Then, scooping her up in his strong, woodcutter's arms and cradling her to him like the child she—at least in some ways—still is, he carries her up the stairs.

•   •   •

But even if those fucking letters explain everything, would knowing change anything? And would the change be for the better?

That's the real question.

•   •   •

Perhaps the little girl should feel shame as he undresses her, shame at being naked in front of her father. Perhaps she should feel that she is too old for him to see her that way. But she lets him because she feels none of these things. She feels nothing. Not even when he lifts her up and lowers her into the almost too hot water of the bath.

And though she feels none of it, he is careful with her, as if she might break.

She is, after all, still such a very little girl.

•   •   •

The garage is as much of a mess as I remember, but the lawnmower is right at the very front, where I knew it would be. Right where he could get at it easily because he liked to keep the lawn neatly mowed. A gas can, old and dented with most of the original bright red paint chipped away, sits on top of it.

•   •   •

Later, as she becomes aware of herself again, she hears noises from downstairs. Hears her father moving around. She will always know the heavy sound of his footsteps. When she hears the door open and then close again, she slips from under the covers of her bed and, in the pajamas her father had dressed her in, creeps down the stairs to the kitchen.

.   .   .

I look behind me in the rearview mirror as I start the car. The fire in the driveway has already burned itself out. All that remains of the two boxes is smoke and ash on the breeze.

The afternoon is growing late, the house falling into shadow as the sun works its way down behind the trees. I'll need to stop and get some real sleep before very long, but I can put at least a couple of hours between here and there before then.

Glancing one last time at the silhouette of the empty house as I turn out of the driveway, it isn't clear if the shutters are green or blue.

Sorry, Susan, but I'm okay with that.

.   .   .

The floor is clean. The knife hangs back on the wall where it has always hung.

Both her father and her older brother are gone.

Grabbing her jacket and boots from beside the door, the little girl runs out into the rain. Into the forest and away from the tiny house where they had all once lived as a happy little family—a mother and a father, and a big brother and his little sister.

Once upon a time.

ABOUT THE AUTHOR

Growing up in "Stephen King Country", Alan P. Marks has long dreamed of becoming a best-selling author (or at least getting a novel published). In the meantime, he teaches at the University of Maine where he has been on faculty for over a quarter century.

After getting his M.A. in Creative Writing there, he simply never left. He teaches courses on writing and literature, including topics such as monsters, the apocalypse, vampires, and (yes) Stephen King. He recently received his MFA in Creative Writing from the Stonecoast program at the University of Southern Maine. He is still working on that elusive first novel.

ALSO BY THE AUTHOR

AND THE CAT CAME BACK

Alan P. Marks

Terrence is a fussy, pretentious little man with terrible allergies and a deep dislike for all things feline.

But that does not mean he ran over Mister Whiskers, his boss's prized cat, on purpose?

Available in digital and trade paperback editions from
Graveside Press
gravesidepress.com

www.ingramcontent.com/pod-product-compliance
Lightning Source LLC
Chambersburg PA
CBHW031453310726
48971CB00003B/900